Little Goat's New Horns

Ariane Chottin
Adapted by Patricia Jensen
Illustrations by Pascale Wirth

Reader's Digest Kids
Pleasantville, N.Y.—Montreal

Little Goat lived on a mountain with her mother and father. One day, as she looked at herself in the clear pond, she noticed something new.

"Mama!" said Little Goat. "My horns are coming in!" Then she sighed. "But they are not nearly as beautiful as yours."

Mama smiled and said, "Soon they will be."

Little Goat scampered off to play with her friend the antelope. The two friends bumped heads to greet each other.

"Look at my new horns!" said Little Goat. "Mama says they will soon be as beautiful as hers."

"My horns are coming in, too," said the antelope. "And when they are fully grown, they will be as beautiful as my father's."

Little Goat looked at the antelope's father, who was standing on a rock. "Those *are* beautiful horns," she said. "They are bigger than mine will ever be."

Suddenly Little Goat didn't feel like playing anymore. She said good-bye and headed home.

On her way, Little Goat noticed the ibex family across the slope. She stared at their long, curved horns.

"Their horns are so long they can scratch their backs with them!" said Little Goat. Then she thought about the horns she would have.

"A goat's horns aren't so beautiful," she said. "I wish I could have different horns."

Little Goat walked on. Soon she saw her friend the fawn.

"Why do you look so unhappy, Little Goat?" asked the fawn.

"It's my horns," Little Goat sighed. "They're so small, and they will never be as beautiful as the other animals' horns."

The fawn shook her head. "I think your horns are coming in very nicely. Besides," she added, "many animals never grow horns at all. I will be a doe when I grow up, and does don't have horns."

Just then the fawn's father walked into the clearing. "There you are," he said to his daughter. "It's time for us to go home."

Little Goat stared at the buck's tremendous antlers. "Oh, my!" she said. "Your antlers are huge! That's what I want!"

“Little Goat,” laughed the fawn, “don’t you think antlers would look silly on a goat?”

“I would never feel silly if I had wonderful antlers like that!” said Little Goat.

When Little Goat arrived home, her grandfather was waiting for her.

"Oh, Grandfather, I'm very sad," she said. "Why can't I have long, curved horns like the ibex, or huge antlers like the buck?"

Her grandfather thought for a minute. "Let me tell you a story," he said. "Then you'll understand."

Once upon a time, a pretty orange bird was flying through a magical forest.

"How beautiful the animals here are!" said the bird. "Each has one long, golden horn. I wish I had a horn just like theirs."

Then one of the animals spoke to the bird. "We are unicorns," it said. "Our horns are perfect for us. But you would look just as silly with a unicorn's horn as we would look with bright orange feathers!"

"I like that story!" said Little Goat. "And it has given me a wonderful idea!"

She bounded off to tell her mother. "Mama! Mama!" she called. "May I have a party for all my friends?"

"What sort of party?" asked Mama.

Little Goat laughed and said, "A party to celebrate my beautiful horns as soon as they have grown in."

The day of the party, all of Little Goat's friends arrived. Mothers and fathers stood off to one side and watched their children play.

No one was more pleased than Little Goat. "Long horns, short horns, or no horns," she said. "It doesn't matter. We can all be happy with who we are."

Goats have very good balance. They can run down steep slopes and climb up steep rocks without stumbling.

A young goat is called a kid. Kids drink their mothers' milk for about a month.

A male goat has a beard under his chin and is sometimes called a billy goat. Female goats are often called nanny goats.